TREASURE OF THE GOLD DRAGON

BY

TRACEY WEST

SCHOLASTIC INC.

DRAGON MASTERS

Read All the Adventures

More books coming soon!

TABLE OF CONTENTS

FOR MY MOM AND DAD, CAROLE AND TOM.

Thanks for inspiring me to become a reader and a writer! — TW

Text copyright © 2019 by Tracey West
Interior illustrations copyright © 2019 Scholastic Inc.

Library of Congress Cataloging-in-Publication Data
Names: West, Tracey, 1965- author. Foresti, Sara, illustrator. | West, Tracey, 1965- Dragon Masters ; 12.
Title: Treasure of the Gold Dragon / by Tracey West ; illustrated by Sara Foresti.
Description: First edition. | New York, NY : Branches/Scholastic Inc., 2019. | Series: Dragon masters ;
12 | Summary: Having taken the silver key, the evil wizard Maldred is after the gold key, which is
protected by the Gold Dragon and her Dragon Master, Darma, but by the time Drake and Rori get there,
Eko and her Thunder Dragon have seized the gold key—so together the three dragon masters, follow her
through the portal to Maldred's tower, but without their dragons will they be able to stop Maldred and
his deluded helper, or even save themselves?
Identifiers: LCCN 2018031376 | ISBN 9781338263688 (pbk) | ISBN 9781338263695 (hardcover)
Subjects: LCSH: Dragons—Juvenile fiction. | Magic—Juvenile fiction. | Wizards—Juvenile fiction.| Locks
and keys—Juvenile fiction. | Adventure stories. | CYAC: Dragons—Fiction. Magic—Fiction.| Wizards—
Fiction. Locks and keys—Fiction. | Adventure and adventurers—Fiction. | GSAFD: Adventure fiction. |
LCGFT: Action and adventure fiction.
Classification: LCC PZ7.W51937 Ts 2019 DDC 813.54 [Fic] —dc23 LC record available at
https://lccn.loc.gov/2018031376

10 9 8 7 6 5 4 3 2 1   19 20 21 22 23

Printed in China 62

First edition, January 2019
Illustrated by Sara Foresti
Edited by Katie Carella
Book design by Jessica Meltzer

A NEW MISSION

In an underground classroom in King Roland's castle, the Dragon Masters were planning to save the world.

Griffith, the royal wizard, stood over a map of the Island of Suvarna. The Dragon Masters — Drake, Rori, Bo, Ana, and Petra — gathered around him.

"You must leave for Suvarna right away," Griffith began. "But let us review what has happened so far. We know that Maldred needs two keys — the Silver Key and the Gold Key — in order to awaken the Naga."

"A huge and powerful dragon who can destroy everything!" Rori piped up.

"Exactly, Rori," Griffith said. "Drake and Bo tried to stop Maldred from stealing the Silver Key. But as you know, Maldred got away with it."

"We are very sorry," said Bo. "We tried our best."

"It wasn't your fault!" Ana cried. "Maldred is the most powerful dark wizard ever!"

I feel like we let everyone down, Drake thought. Then he said, "We will not let Maldred get the Gold Key!"

"Maldred is on his way to steal it now," Griffith said. "The Gold Key is kept in the Gold Lair. The lair is hidden inside a mountain on the Island of Suvarna. And it is guarded by the Gold Dragon."

"We need to leave," Rori said, tapping her foot. "Maldred could have the key by now!"

"I fear you may be right," Griffith said. "Drake, please ask Worm to transport you, Rori, and Vulcan to Suvarna. I need the others to stay with me for a special mission."

"Yes!" Rori cheered. "I get to go!"

Petra gave Rori a hug. "Good luck, and be safe," she said.

Drake and Rori hurried to the Dragon Caves.

Drake looked at his big, brown Earth Dragon. "Are you ready, Worm?"

The green stone that Drake wore around his neck began to glow. It was a piece of the Dragon Stone, the magical stone that had chosen all the Dragon Masters.  Every Dragon Master wore a small piece of it. Their stones glowed when their dragons communicated with them.

Drake heard Worm's voice inside his head. *I am ready.*

"We're all set!" Drake told Rori.

Then Rori put one hand on Vulcan, her red Fire Dragon. She put her other hand on Worm.

Drake smiled at Worm. "Please transport us to the mountain that Griffith showed us!"

Worm's body began to glow green. The light became brighter. Drake felt his stomach flip-flop.

When the light faded, they were standing on a rocky mountain ledge. The air felt warm on Drake's skin. Drake looked up.

The Gold Dragon flew across the sky. A dark-haired boy rode on her back. Drake's mouth dropped open at the sight of the dragon. Shining gold scales covered her whole body. Her wings curled and reminded him of bird feathers. She was beautiful!

But then Drake heard a loud roar in the sky.

Booooooooooooom!

It sounded like thunder.

He turned. A purple Thunder Dragon was chasing the Gold Dragon! A woman with black hair rode on the back of the purple dragon. Drake knew them both.

He gasped.

"It's Eko and Neru!" he cried.

"Look! There's something in Eko's hand," Rori said. She squinted. "It's the Gold Key!"

BATTLE IN THE SKY

Drake shaded his eyes with his hand. The sun made the scales of the Gold Dragon shine brightly. He also noticed a gold object glittering in Eko's hand. Rori was right. It looked like the Gold Key!

Not long ago, Eko had tried to steal Worm and the other dragons from King Roland's castle. Rori had left to live with her for a short while, before learning Eko was not a *good* Dragon Master ...

"Is Eko helping Maldred now?" Drake wondered out loud.

"Maybe. Or maybe she wants the Gold Key to herself," Rori replied. "Either way, we can't let her take it!"

Rori jumped onto Vulcan's back. "Vulcan, fly!" she said.

Then she and her dragon flew through the portal right before it vanished.

"Nooo!" Rori cried.

She and Vulcan flew down and landed next to Drake and Worm. The Gold Dragon and the dark-haired boy set down slowly and gracefully beside them.

"Vulcan, break the shield!" Rori yelled as they flew closer to the Thunder Dragon.

Vulcan shot a ball of flame from his mouth. It hit the shield but didn't break it.

Neru roared loudly.

A portal of swirling energy opened up in the blue sky. Eko looked at Rori and laughed.

Will the Gold Lair look anything like the Silver Lair? he wondered. The Silver Lair had been filled with piles of amazing treasures!

Soon they heard the sound of running water. They came to a small waterfall.

Darma motioned for the others to follow him. Then he stepped behind the waterfall. Drake, Rori, and the dragons followed.

Darma and his dragon began to walk up the mountain. Drake and Rori followed. As they walked, the silver sword tucked into Drake's belt felt heavy. Jean, the Dragon Master of the Silver Dragon, had given it to him.

Drake turned to Worm. "Can you transport us up there so we can get the key from Eko?" he asked.

Neru's shield is too strong, Worm replied. *I cannot transport past it.*

Drake looked up. The Thunder Dragon's body glowed with purple energy, forming an energy shield around him and Eko.

The Gold Dragon shot golden beams from her eyes.

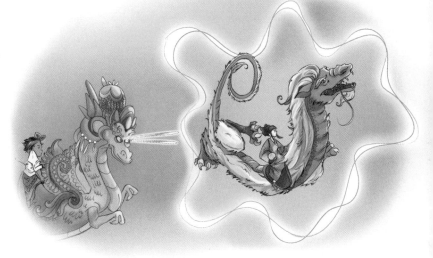

The golden beams hit Neru's shield and bounced off.

The Fire Dragon flapped his huge wings and flew toward the two dragons in the sky.

WAS THAT MAGIC?

Rori stepped closer to Darma. "How can you be so calm?" she asked, her voice rising. "If Eko is working with Maldred, that means he has both keys! He will be able to release the Naga and destroy the world!"

"Who is Maldred?" Darma asked.

"He is a dark wizard," Rori replied. "The baddest guy you'll ever meet."

For a moment, Drake forgot about Eko and stared in wonder at the Gold Dragon.

The boy climbed down. He wore a white shirt and a skirt with a dragon pattern on it. Around his neck, he wore a green Dragon Stone.

"I am Darma," he said. "And this is Hema, the Gold Dragon. We are the guardians of the Gold Key."

"We know the Thunder Dragon's Dragon Master, Eko," Rori said. "Did she just get away with the Gold Key?"

Darma nodded. "She did," he said. "The Gold Key is gone."

Darma closed his eyes. After a few seconds, he opened them. "We can still stop him," he said calmly.

"How do you know that?" Rori asked.

Drake decided to step in. "I'm Drake," he told Darma. "This is my dragon, Worm. And this is Rori and her dragon, Vulcan."

Darma nodded. "It is nice to meet you," he said.

"You, too," Drake said. "We knew Maldred was coming here to steal the Gold Key. I'm sorry we didn't get here in time."

Darma smiled. "That is okay. You are here now."

Rori interrupted. "We have to figure out where Eko went!" She turned to Darma. "Were Eko's eyes glazed over red?"

Darma shook his head. "They were not."

Rori frowned. "I thought maybe Maldred put her under a spell," she said. "But I guess he didn't. So if Eko is helping him, it's because she wants to. But why?"

"Does it matter?" Drake asked. "She has the key now. She probably took it to wherever his hiding place is."

"Right," Rori agreed. "We need to find Maldred's hideout and get there fast!"

Darma spoke up again, in his soft, calm voice. "I know how to find Eko," he said. "Follow me, please."

The tunnel opened up into a big, bright room lit by torches. Gold lined the walls. Dozens of gold treasure chests glittered in the torchlight. A large gold platform topped with big, fluffy gold pillows sat in the center of the room.

The Gold Dragon must sleep there, Drake guessed.

Darma smiled. "Welcome to the lair of the Gold Dragon!"

They were inside a damp, cool cavern. Six golden dragon statues, each as tall as the Dragon Masters, formed a circle in the center.

"They're beautiful," Rori whispered.

Darma walked up to one of the statues. He pulled down on the dragon's tail, and a door slid open on the cavern wall.

Darma led them through the door, into a dark tunnel. Drake couldn't see a thing. They walked for a few minutes.

CHAPTER 4

GOLDEN TREASURES

"This is a nice lair," Rori said, tapping her foot. "But we need to find out where Eko went!"

Darma nodded. He walked over to the wall on the right, and then stopped.

"Eko and the Thunder Dragon entered the lair through this wall," he said. "That is how she broke in and stole the Gold Key."

"Neru can make portals when he roars," Drake explained.

"The portal is not here anymore, but magical portals have a great deal of energy," Darma said. "They usually leave some energy behind."

"Are you saying you think we can still travel through Neru's portal, even though we can't see it?" Rori asked.

Darma closed his eyes and held up his hand, with his open palm facing the wall. Then he began to move his hand in a circle.

A slowly swirling circle of purple energy began to appear in the wall.

"The portal!" Rori cried.

Drake gasped. "Are you sure you're a Dragon Master and not a wizard?" he asked.

Darma smiled. "It is easy to find energy, if you know where to look," he said. "The portal will close very soon. But before we leave, I must give you each something."

Darma opened one of the treasure chests. He took out a red jewel hanging from a gold chain. He gave it to Rori.

"This is for you," he said.

"Uh, thanks," Rori replied, and she slipped the chain over her head.

Then Darma walked to a different treasure chest. He pulled out a vest made of gold chain mail. He handed it to Drake. "Please put this on."

Drake put the vest on over his shirt. It felt a lot lighter than he thought it would. "Thank you," he said. "But why have you given us these gifts?"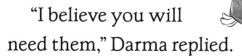

"I believe you will need them," Darma replied.

"For what?" Rori asked.

"We will know when the time comes," he replied.

Darma walked back to the portal. He held his hand against it. Then he turned back to Drake and Rori.

"The portal's energy is weak," he said. "Not all of us will be able to travel through it. The dragons must stay here."

"What?!" Rori cried. "How can we fight Maldred and Eko without our dragons?"

"We will find a way," Darma replied.

Drake turned to Worm. *I do not want to leave you behind, Worm,* he said in his mind. His Dragon Stone glowed, and he heard Worm's voice inside his head.

Follow Darma. Find the Gold Key. Time is running out.

"Worm says we should go," Drake told Rori.

Rori sighed. "Fine," she said. "Then let's do this."

She pushed past Darma and stepped through the portal. The two boys followed her.

THE WIZARD'S PLAN

The portal quickly disappeared behind the three Dragon Masters. They stepped into a tall, round tower. A spiral staircase led down to many floors below.

Torches mounted on the walls lit up the space. The light was dim, but Drake could make out strange faces painted on the wall. The hairs on the back of his neck stood up at the sight of them.

Then Rori tugged on his arm. She put a finger to her lips and pointed down. At the bottom of the tower, a wizard dressed in a red robe stood at a big desk. He had a long, black beard with a white stripe. And he wore an eye patch over one eye.

"It's Maldred!" Rori whispered.

"This must be his secret hideout," Darma said. "And that must be his workshop. Look at all the books and potions down there."

Drake peered over the railing. Maldred was five floors below them. Drake could see that walkways broke off the staircase and circled around the tower all the way down. There were doors on each of the floors.

This is a huge hideout! he thought. *Where in the world are we?*

Down below, Eko walked up to the desk. She held a gold disc with unusual markings on it. It glittered in the candlelight.

She is *working with Maldred!* Drake thought.

Eko handed over the Gold Key. "Maldred, I have brought you the key," she said.

The wizard smiled. "You did well, Eko," he said.

"And now, together, we will release the Naga," Eko said. "We will create a world where dragons can be free."

Drake had heard Eko say something like this before. When Eko had tried to steal King Roland's dragons, she had claimed that she wanted all dragons to be free. She didn't believe that dragons should have Dragon Masters.

Maldred held up the Silver Key. "Now I have both keys," he said. "But I still do not know where to find the Naga. I have read every page of *The Lore of the Ancient One*, but the book does not tell me where the Naga lives."

He angrily slammed his fist on the desk.

"Perhaps the answer lies in the keys," Eko suggested. "They have markings on them."

Maldred raised an eyebrow. "You may be right," he said. "I will need to study them."

"Let me help," Eko said.

"There is one way you can help me," Maldred told her. "Keep an eye out for Griffith's Dragon Masters. We cannot let them stop us from waking the Naga. If you see them, show them no mercy."

"But we can't hurt them, Maldred," Eko said. "They're just children."

Maldred stared at her. "I said no mercy," he repeated. "Nothing must stop my dream of ruling the world."

"You mean *our* dream — of freeing the dragons," Eko said.

Maldred smiled. "Of course, my dear, of course."

Rori whispered loudly to Drake. "Does Eko really think Maldred's going to set the dragons free? He's tricking her. He wants the dragons for himself!"

"Shhh," Drake warned.

Suddenly, Rori yelled, "Don't trust him, Eko!"

MALDRED'S HELPER

Maldred's head snapped up. His eye fixed on the Dragon Masters at the top of the tower.

"Darma, quick!" Drake cried. "Open the portal again!"

Drake turned around, but he didn't see Darma anywhere.

"Darma?" he called out.

Rori grabbed Drake's arm. "We have to hide!" she said. "Let's get to one of the tower rooms. Maybe there is a window we can climb out of."

Drake and Rori raced down the spiral staircase. Drake's heart pounded.

Then, from the corner of his eye, he saw a flutter of red fabric. Maldred floated up toward them, his body glowing with red energy.

"Two Dragon Masters, how nice!" he said with an evil laugh. "You are like mice in a trap!"

"You can't catch us!" Rori cried, still racing down the steps.

Maldred pointed at Drake and Rori, extending his long fingers. "Of course I can," he said. "I am a wizard!"

Suddenly, Drake felt his whole body tingle. "I . . . I can't move!" he cried.

"Me neither!" Rori yelled.

"No, you cannot," he said. "So you won't be needing your sword anymore."

Drake watched helplessly as his silver sword floated out of his belt and into Maldred's hands.

Then Eko came running up the staircase.

"Lock them up, Eko!" Maldred ordered. "I will deal with them later!"

Eko grabbed Drake and Rori. Maldred snapped his long fingers, and Drake felt the tingling stop.

TRAPPED!

Rori started pounding on the door.

"Let us out of here!" she yelled.

Drake looked around. The room was bare except for a rickety wood table and a water jug. An eerie glow streamed through the bars of a tiny window high up on the wall.

"I'll try to contact Worm," he said. "I know he is back in the Gold Lair, but maybe I can connect with him. Maybe he can help us escape."

Drake closed his eyes.

Worm, can you hear me? he asked.

Drake opened his eyes and looked down at his Dragon Stone. It didn't glow at all. He sighed. "We'll have to find a way out of here on our own."

Rori pushed the table over to the window and stood on top of it. Drake held the table steady.

"It looks so weird out there," Rori said. "Glowy and strange." She yanked on the bars.

"It's no use!" she cried. She jumped down from the table. "We're trapped!"

"Maybe not," Drake said. "Darma has got to be inside this tower somewhere. Maybe he'll come and save us."

"He's probably in some kind of trouble, too," Rori said.

Drake slumped down on the floor. "Maldred can't keep us in here forever," he said. "We'll just have to escape the next time he or Eko comes to open the door."

"That's if anyone comes at all," Rori said, sliding down to sit beside him. "They might leave us here until Maldred and the Naga destroy the world."

"Or maybe Maldred will come and put a dark spell on us — to force us to help with his evil plan," Drake said.

The two Dragon Masters got quiet, thinking about this.

"I will keep trying to contact Worm," Drake said finally.

He held his Dragon Stone, closed his eyes, and tried again. And again.

Worm didn't respond. Drake started to worry.

We're separated from our dragons. Darma is missing. And Maldred has my sword, he thought. *There is no way we can stop Maldred now!*

RUN!

few minutes later, the door creaked
open. Drake and Rori jumped to their feet.
Someone shoved a tray into the room, then
quickly closed the door.

Drake and Rori ran over and pounded on
the door.

"Let us out! Let us out!" they shouted.

They yelled until their throats were sore.

Then Drake looked down at the tray. It held bread, cheese, apples, and two mugs of water. His stomach rumbled.

"I'm starving," he said.

Rori watched as Drake ate bread and cheese. Then she took some herself. They sat on the floor and ate until every crumb was gone, except for the apple cores.

Drake suddenly felt very tired.

Of course I'm tired, he thought. *I haven't slept in a really long time!*

"Let's get some sleep," he said. "If Maldred does try to hurt us, we'll need our energy."

"I'll stay awake and guard us," Rori said, but she yawned, too.

Drake leaned back against the wall and dozed off. He wasn't sure how long he had slept for when a voice awakened him.

"Get up!"

Eko stood over him and Rori, who had also fallen asleep. The door to their cell was open.

"Wake up," Eko said. "Maldred wants to see you."

Drake and Rori stretched and stood up. Eko, who stood behind them, pushed them forward.

Rori looked at Drake and mouthed one word.

Run.

THE SECRET OF THE KEYS

Drake and Rori dashed through the open door and raced to the spiral staircase. They bounded down the steps to the next walkway and headed for the nearest door.

Before they could reach it, two glowing red orbs appeared in front of them.

The glowing orbs quickly surrounded the Dragon Masters. Drake's skin prickled as both orbs floated down to Maldred's workshop.

They landed in front of Maldred. Drake noticed his silver sword propped up against the workshop wall.

Pop! The orbs burst like bubbles, freeing Drake and Rori.

Eko ran into the room. "I am sorry, Maldred," she said. "They surprised me."

Maldred scowled at her. "I need you to keep a better watch over my prisoners," he said. "I am going to need them."

"What do you need us for?" Rori asked.

"Let me show you what I've discovered," Maldred said, rubbing his hands together. "I was staring at the markings on the keys when it came to me. Watch!"

He picked up the silver disc and pressed it into a dish of black ink. Then he pressed the disc onto a clean sheet of white paper. The raised markings on the key were stamped on the paper.

"Now the Gold Key," he said, and he repeated the process. He stamped the Gold Key right on top of the design left by the Silver Key.

Rori gasped. "That looks like a map!" she cried.

"Exactly," Maldred said. Then he covered the paper so Rori and Drake couldn't see it. "I recognize the islands on it. Now I know where to find the Naga!"

"You can't do this!" Rori yelled. "You can't destroy the world!"

"I don't want to destroy it," Maldred said. "I want to rule it! Everyone will bow down to me with the Naga by my side!"

As Maldred cackled, Drake spotted something out of the corner of his eye. A flash of gold, moving along a bookshelf. He blinked. It looked like a mouse — a gold mouse! He blinked again, and the creature was gone.

How strange, Drake thought.

"You still haven't said what you need us for," Rori said to Maldred.

"I learned something very interesting in this book. When I summon the Naga, he will be *very* hungry," the dark wizard said, and his eye glittered as he grinned at Drake and Rori. "And I know the perfect snack for a giant, hungry dragon!"

EKO MAKES A CHOICE

You can't feed us to the Naga!" Drake yelled at Maldred.

Rori stomped over to Eko. "Did you hear that? Do you still want to help him?"

Eko looked at Maldred. "Surely, Maldred, you cannot be serious," she said. "It is not necessary to harm the children."

The dark wizard scowled at her. "*I* shall decide what is necessary," he said. "As long as the Dragon Masters live, they will try to stop us. This will solve that problem."

"Let me watch over them, Maldred," Eko argued. "They won't escape from me again."

While Eko talked, Rori grabbed Drake's hand. They slowly backed away from Eko and Maldred. First one step. Then two. Then three.

Then Rori signaled Drake by squeezing his hand, and they both dashed away from Maldred and Eko.

Maldred pointed at Rori and Drake, and sizzling red lightning shot from his fingertip.

Drake felt a jolt go through his body. Then he realized he wasn't moving. Maldred had frozen them!

"Don't you see? You can't escape me!" Maldred said. "I shall cast a spell on you both, putting you under my control. That will keep you out of trouble until it's feeding time!"

Maldred moved his finger, and Drake saw Rori float through the air toward the wizard. She stopped right in front of him.

"Look at me, Rori," Maldred commanded.

She's frozen just like I am, Drake thought. Soon, her eyes will glaze over red and she'll be under Maldred's control. Then I'll be next.

"I can't let you do this, Maldred!" Eko cried. She shoved him away from Rori, sending him sprawling on the floor.

Drake felt the magical hold release him. He and Rori dropped to the ground.

"Enough, Eko!" Maldred said as he rose to his feet. "I don't need you anymore!"

He dipped his hand into his pocket and came up with a handful of sparkling red dust. He tossed the dust at Eko.

The red dust sparkled, and Eko disappeared!

A SPELL IS CAST

Rori yelled at Maldred. "Where did you send Eko? What did you do with her?"

Maldred just grinned. "Now, where were we?" he asked.

He zapped Drake and Rori again with his red lightning. Once more, Rori floated in front of his face.

Nooooo! Drake thought. He struggled to move, but he was frozen.

Maldred stared into Rori's eyes and chanted: *"Your will is gone. Your will is mine. Your will is gone. Your will is mine."*

Rori closed her eyes and nodded.

Rori, nooooo! Drake yelled inside his head.

Then Rori floated to the ground.

Maldred zapped her again to unfreeze her.

Next, he pointed at Drake. Drake floated through the air and stopped right in front of Maldred. The wizard stared at him with his black, glittering eye.

"Your turn, Drake," Maldred said.

Drake tried to close his eyes. To resist. But he couldn't even move his eyelids.

"Your will is gone," Maldred chanted. *"Your will is mine."*

"No, it isn't!" Rori cried.

She grabbed a bubbling potion from Maldred's table and tossed it in the wizard's face! Maldred screamed as purple smoke billowed from his beard.

Somehow, Rori escaped Maldred's spell, Drake thought as he dropped to the floor. He wasn't frozen anymore. Rori helped him up.

They dashed upstairs and ran down the walkway. They entered the first room they found. Inside was a large window with wooden shutters. Rori and Drake ran to it.

"The shutters are locked," Drake said, pulling on them.

Rori stepped up next to him and tried to help him pry them open. That's when Drake noticed that the red jewel around her neck was glowing.

"Look at the jewel Darma gave you!" he said.

"It started to glow when Maldred was putting that spell on me," Rori replied. "I think that's why the spell didn't work. The jewel protected me."

"But you really looked like you were under Maldred's control," Drake said.

She smiled. "I know. I fooled him pretty good."

"Darma knew what he was doing when he gave you that necklace," Drake said. Then he remembered the golden mouse. "And I have a feeling he's still going to help us somehow."

They turned back to the shutters just as Maldred stepped into the room.

"You cannot escape!" He cackled, and red lightning flew from his fingertips.

RESCUED!

Drake and Rori dodged the wizard's lightning blast. Then —

Aaaaiiiiiiiieeeeeeeeeeeeeeeee! A strange cry filled the tower.

A golden eagle flew into the room! The large bird picked up Maldred in her claws and flew away with him.

Drake and Rori looked at each other, their eyes wide.

"Let's get out of here!" Rori said, turning back to the window.

"Not yet," Drake said. "I think we should follow that eagle!"

If that eagle is who I think it is, she might need our help, he thought.

Drake ran out of the room. Rori sighed and ran after him.

The large eagle flew down to Maldred's workshop. Maldred squirmed in her sharp golden claws. Darma stood there. He was holding the Silver Key and the Gold Key!

"Those keys are mine!" Maldred yelled. His legs dangled over the floor.

"They are not yours," Darma replied. "They were never yours. We must keep them safe."

"I will do everything in my power to get those keys back!" Maldred said.

"You will not get them back," Darma said.

"We've got to lock Maldred up!" Rori told Darma.

Darma looked up at the golden eagle. "Hema, make sure Maldred can't move."

I knew it! Drake thought. *The eagle* is *Hema!*

The eagle set Maldred down. Before
he could run away, she shot streams of
golden energy from her mouth. The
energy wrapped around the wizard like a
rope. He couldn't move.

Drake turned to Darma. "We've got to get those keys out of here," he said.

"There appears to be no escape from this hideout," Darma replied. "It is located in some kind of magical space."

"So *that's* why it looks weird and glowy outside," Rori said.

Maldred cackled. "You cannot escape, and you can't stop me," he said. "When will you Dragon Masters learn? I don't need my *hands* to do magic. I only need the power of my mind!"

Suddenly, an army of red orbs appeared in the workshop. The orbs zoomed through the air, wildly shooting around the space.

Rori dove under the desk. Drake moved to follow her, when one of the red orbs zoomed right toward him.

"Drake!" Rori yelled.

GOLD VS. RED

The red orb hit Drake in the chest.

Drake had seen Maldred's red orbs take down strong palace guards. He knew how powerful they could be. He expected to be sent flying. But the orb bounced right off him!

How am I not hurt? he wondered, touching his chest. Then he felt the gold chain-mail vest Darma had given him. *The gold vest protected me!*

Angry, Maldred scowled at Drake. The wizard's whole body began to glow with red energy. The gold energy that was wrapped around him dissolved into glittering dust.

Maldred pointed at Darma and sent a red orb flying toward him. The orb surrounded Darma, and he began to float toward Maldred.

"Those keys are mine!" the wizard yelled.

Rori climbed out from under the desk and ran toward Darma.

At the same time, a golden light exploded from the eagle! The light filled the room. When it faded, Hema the Gold Dragon stood there.

The dragon's eyes flashed. She roared and shot golden beams at Maldred.

The dark wizard held up both palms and created a red energy shield in front of him. The dragon's beams hit the shield but couldn't break through it. The red energy absorbed them.

"Rooooar!" Hema couldn't break through Maldred's shield.

Instead, she turned and hit a blast of gold energy at the orb surrounding Darma. The red orb burst, and Darma tumbled to the floor. The Silver Key and the Gold Key flew out of his hands.

"The keys!" Rori cried, and she dove after them.

But Maldred was closer. He scooped up the two keys.

Then he sprinkled sparkling red dust on top of his head.

In a flash, he disappeared, and the red orbs popped like bubbles.

THE MAGIC OF THE SWORD

Maldred got away!" Rori yelled. "He knows where the Naga is, and now he's going to destroy the world! We've got to go after him!"

"But we don't know where the Naga is," Drake said, and he felt tears sting his eyes. "We failed."

"You have not failed yet," Darma said. "We *do* know where the Naga is."

The boy held up a map — the map Maldred had made using the two keys.

Drake's eyes got wide. "It looks like those islands make the shape of a dragon. We've got to show this to Griffith. He'll know where those islands are."

Rori looked at Darma. "How did you get Maldred's map?"

Darma grinned. "A little mouse brought it to me," he said, and he looked at Hema.

"I knew it!" Drake cried.

"Hema can change into other animals — not just an eagle?" Rori asked.

"Yes," Darma replied. "She can transform into anything — from a tiny bee to a large elephant."

"Whoa!" Drake cried. "That's an awesome power!"

"It is," Rori agreed. Then she frowned. "But how did Hema get into the hideout? I thought you said dragons couldn't make it through the portal."

"That was true. The portal's energy was weak. Hema transformed into a mouse, so she was small enough to come through," Darma answered.

"That explains a lot. But where have you been?" Drake asked.

"Yeah, where were you when we were getting captured?" Rori added.

"By the time we entered the hideout, I could sense we were about to be discovered," Darma replied.

"If you *sensed* that, why didn't you warn us?" Rori asked.

"I'm sorry. Everything happened quickly," Darma replied. "I knew I would have a better chance of helping us if I was not seen. So I hid."

"You saved us from Maldred, so I guess you did the right thing," Drake said.

"I guess so," Rori said. "But Maldred still got away."

"We have to get back to the Gold Lair," Drake said. "Worm can transport us all back to Bracken from there."

"Are you forgetting something?" Rori asked. "We're, like, trapped in this hideout in some magical space or something."

"Rori is right," Darma said. "We need a portal to get out of here. But we have no way to make one."

Drake sighed as he walked across the room and picked up the silver sword. "At least I have my sword back."

Darma's eyes widened. "Is that from the Silver Dragon's lair?"

Drake nodded. "Yes. Jean — the Silver Dragon's Dragon Master — gave it to me."

"The silver and gold treasures are all connected to the dragons who guard them," Darma said. "I think you may be able to use your sword to make a portal that takes us to the Silver Dragon."

"That would get us out of here!" Rori said. "And then Drake could contact Worm!"

"I get it," Drake said. "But how do I open a portal?"

"Make a circle in the air with your sword," Darma replied.

Drake held the silver sword in both hands and made a big circle.

"Again," Darma said. "Keep going!"

Drake made circle after circle.

Finally, the air began to swirl with silver light. A new portal appeared.

"You did it!" Rori cheered, and Drake grinned at her.

"Excellent!" Darma said, and he and Hema stepped through the portal.

SILVER AND GOLD

rake and Rori followed Darma and Hema
through the portal.

Drake blinked.

Argent, the shining Silver Dragon, stood in front of them. Jean, his Dragon Master, grinned at Drake. But they were not in the Silver Lair. They were in the Gold Lair!

Drake was confused. "Argent? Jean?" he asked. "What are you doing here?"

"As soon as our king gave us leave, we came to join you and take back the Silver Key," she answered. "Argent tracked the silver sword here, where we found Worm and Vulcan waiting for you."

"Worm!" Drake cried, and he ran to his dragon. Then he turned back to Jean. "We were inside Maldred's hideout! Eko was there. We tried to get the keys back, but he has both of them now. The Silver Key and the Gold Key."

Jean frowned. "That is bad news. But we will stop him."

Rori patted Vulcan's neck and looked at Jean. "So you're Jean," she said. "Nice armor."

"Thanks," Jean said. "You must be Rori. Worm told Argent all about you."

Darma nodded to Jean. "It is nice to meet you, Guardian of the Silver Key. I am Darma, Guardian of the Gold Key."

Jean smiled. "We both thought we would never leave our lairs. And now look at us!"

"There will be time to get to know one another later," Rori said. "Maldred has both keys. We have to find him and stop him!"

"Rori is right," Jean agreed, and Rori raised her eyebrows. Jean went on, "Maldred must be headed to the location of the Naga. Did you find out where that is?"

Darma showed her the map. "Somewhere in this group of islands," he said.

"Griffith will know where those islands are," Drake said. "We need to get back to Bracken. All the Dragon Masters will have to work together to find the Naga and stop Maldred."

"Yes, we must," Darma agreed.

Drake put one hand on Worm. "Shall we transport?"

Rori and Jean touched their dragons. Darma touched Hema then all the Dragon Masters touched Worm.

"Worm, take us to Bracken!" Drake cried. "Time is running out!"

TRACEY WEST had a challenging time coming up with powers for the Gold Dragon. Then she learned that, more than any other metal, gold can change its shape without breaking. That gave her the idea to make Hema a shape-shifter.

Tracey has written dozens of books for kids. She writes in the house she shares with her husband, her three stepkids (when they're home from college), and her animal friends. She has three dogs, a flock of chickens, and one cat, who sits on her desk when she writes. Thankfully, the cat does not weigh as much as a dragon!

SARA FORESTI was born in Northern Italy, a place surrounded by many beautiful lakes, fields, and rivers. When she was a young girl, her favorite place to visit was a medieval city built on a hill. It was protected by stone walls and tall gates.

Once Sara grew up, she discovered the amazing world of illustration. And she fell in love with it! Sara now works as a children's book illustrator. Her own personal dragon — a very polite Great Dane named Era — watches her while she works.

DRAGON MASTERS
TREASURE OF THE GOLD DRAGON

Questions and Activities

Darma gives Drake and Rori each a gift. What does he give them? How do these gifts help the Dragon Masters?

A SIMILE uses the words "like" or "as" to compare two things. On page 37 Maldred uses a simile when he says Drake and Rori are "like mice in a trap." Can you think of another simile to describe the Dragon Masters in this moment?

Why does Maldred need the Gold and Silver Keys to find the Naga? What does he do with the keys on pages 52–53?

On page 60, Maldred makes Eko disappear. What do **YOU** think happened to her?

Darma's dragon, Hema, has the power to transform into other animals. What animal would you like to transform into?

scholastic.com/branches